Something Queer at the Library

YEARLING BOOKS/YOUNG YEARLINGS/YEARLING CLASSICS are designed especially to entertain and enlighten young people. Patricia Reilly Giff, consultant to this series, received her bachelor's degree from Marymount College and a master's degree in history from St. John's University. She holds a Professional Diploma in Reading and a Doctorate of Humane Letters from Hofstra University. She was a teacher and reading consultant for many years, and is the author of numerous books for young readers.

(a mystery)

something queer at the Library

by
Elizabeth Levy
illustrated by
Mordicai Gerstein

A Young Yearling Book

Published by
Dell Publishing
a division of
Bantam Doubleday Dell Publishing Group, Inc.
1540 Broadway
New York, New York 10036

ISBN: 0-440-48120-1

Reprinted by arrangement with Delacorte Press

Printed in the United States of America

June 1988

20   19   18   17   16   15

CWO

"The All-State Dog Show is next week," Jill explained to Mr. Hobart, the librarian. "We're going to show Fletcher. He's a pure-bred basset hound, but he's never been in a dog show. We need these books to learn how to train him."

"They're oversized books. Usually, I'd ask you to read them here," said Mr. Hobart. "But we're about to close, so I'll let you sign them out for one week. You must take good care of them."

"We promise," said Gwen and Jill.

"I can trust you," said Mr. Hobart. "Good luck!"

MR. HOBART

LIBRARY STAMP

GWEN'S LIBRARY CARD

Fletcher was sleeping under a tree outside the library. Gwen and Jill untied him and hurried home. Fletcher didn't want to hurry. Fletcher never wanted to hurry.

When they got home, Fletcher went to sleep again. Gwen and Jill opened the books.

"Look!" cried Jill. "Somebody's cut out a picture."

"Some pictures are missing in this one, too," said Gwen.

Quickly they leafed through the other books. In each one, a few pictures were cut out. "This is terrible!" said Jill. "What a horrible, creepy thing to do!"

"I think a little kid did it," said Gwen. "The edges are ragged." She paused. "The library's closed for the weekend. We can't take the books back until Monday. Mr. Hobart might think we did it."

"But we promised him we'd take care of them," said Jill. She was upset. "He trusted us."

GWEN THINKING OF MR. HOBART THINKING OF JILL AND GWEN.

Gwen looked at the books on the floor. Then she looked at Jill. "We're going to have to catch the creep who did this ourselves." Gwen started to tap her braces. She always tapped her braces whenever something queer was going on. "I bet there's a clue in the books somewhere," she said.

TAP TAP TAP TAP TAP TAP TAP TAP

GWEN, TAPPING ON THOSE → BRACES

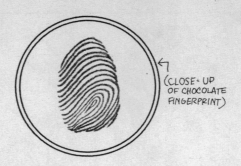

(CLOSE·UP
OF CHOCOLATE
FINGERPRINT)

They went over the books page by page. "I found something," shrieked Jill. "A fingerprint! The creep was eating chocolate and left a fingerprint. You can see the swirls. We've got him—or her."

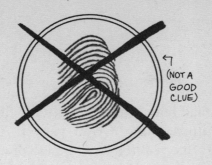
(NOT A GOOD CLUE)

"Jill," said Gwen. "A fingerprint doesn't do us any good. We're not the police."

"We could take it to them," insisted Jill.

"It doesn't prove anything. It could have been left by anybody. There must be more clues. Let's keep looking."

A half hour went by, but they didn't find anything. Then Gwen yelled, "Look at this!" She pointed to a strange drawing of a dog on the margin of the page.

CLOSE-UP
OF FUNNY LOOKING
DRAWING

"It's silly looking," said Jill.

"It's a better clue than the fingerprint," said Gwen, tapping her braces. "I bet whoever did it always draws dogs like that. We'll trace it on a piece of paper and ask if anybody has seen a drawing like it before."

Gwen and Jill showed the drawing to all of their friends.

They looked at all the art work on the walls in school.
Nothing matched the dog doodle.

By Wednesday, they had made no progress.

"It's hopeless," said Jill.

"But we can't give up," said Gwen.

"What about the dog show?" asked Jill. "We haven't even started to train Fletcher. If he wins, at least we'll have money to pay for the books."

"We shouldn't have to pay," said Gwen angrily. "The creep who did it should pay."

Gwen and Jill tried to teach Fletcher how to behave
a dog show. He was supposed to stand straight with
s nose in the air.
He was supposed to run at Jill's side in a steady gait.

When Fletcher tried to stand, his nose and belly drooped.

THE RIGHT WAY

FLETCHER'S WAY

THE RIGHT WAY

FLETCHER'S WAY

He kept tripping when he tried to run.
Fletcher was very good at lying down on command.

On Friday, Gwen said, "It's no use. Fletcher will never win."

"Basset hounds are supposed to droop," said Jill, trying to sound hopeful.

Gwen shook her head back and forth. "To-morrow, after the dog show, we have to take the books back to Mr. Hobart. He'll think we did it. This has been one of the worst weeks of my life!"

"Maybe we missed something in the books," suggested Jill. "Let's look again."

Gwen shrugged her shoulders, but they went inside and looked at each book. Suddenly Gwen began to go tap,

tap,

tap on her braces.

"You've found something," cried Jill.

"Look at the captions underneath each missing picture," said Gwen. "They all say Lhasa apso. Sounds like a weird dog food. Do you know what it is?"

"I never heard of it," said Jill.

Lhasa Apso

"We've got to find out. Let's go to the library," said Gwen.

They ran all the way. Fletcher was exhausted when they got there.

"Hi, Gwen and Jill," said Mr. Hobart when he saw them. "Did you bring back the books?"

"They're not due till tomorrow," said Gwen, turning a deep red.

"Is there something wrong?" asked Mr. Hobart. He looked puzzled.

"Oh no," stammered Gwen. "We just have to look something up in the encyclopedia."

"Now he'll really suspect us," whispered Jill. "Why did you have to turn all red?"

"I couldn't help it," whispered Gwen.

L

THE CITY OF LHASA

They got the L volume and looked up Lhasa. It was the capital of Tibet. They found out that Lhasa apso was a funny-looking little dog that originally came from Tibet. Apso meant barking lion in the Tibetan language, so Lhasa apso was a tiny barking lion from Tibet.

LHASA APSO

A SMALL LION   A LARGE LHASA APSO

Gwen sat down on the floor between the stacks and started tapping her braces. "Let's make a list of everything we know about the creep," she said.

1. eats chocolate (maybe)
2. draws dog doodles
3. cuts out pictures of Lhasa apsos

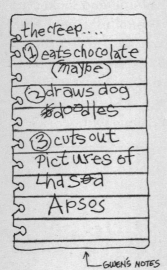

the creep....
① eats chocolate (maybe)
② draws dog ~~doodles~~ doodles
③ cuts out Pictures of Lhasa Apsos

↑ GWEN'S NOTES

"The dog show!" shouted Gwen.

"*Shhh,*" said Jill. "We're in the library. What about the dog show?"

"Those lopsided watchamacallits will be at the dog show," explained Gwen. "I bet the creep will be there, too!"

A LOPSIDED LHASA APSO

The next morning was the start of the dog show. Gwen and Jill gave Fletcher a bath. They combed and brushed him, and practiced running him around in a circle.

Then they hurried to the show.

DOG SHOW

When they got there, Gwen said, "You stay with Fletcher. I'm going to look around. Keep your eye out for any kids eating chocolate."

Gwen found the section reserved for Lhasa apsos. After a while a boy came by eating chocolate raisins. His fingers were covered with chocolate. Gwen started to follow him and almost bumped into a girl eating a Three Musketeers candy bar. Her hands were smeared with chocolate, too.

BOY ← - - - - - - - → GIRL

Gwen didn't know what to do. The girl stopped and looked at the Lhasa apsos. The boy started to walk away. The girl took out a pad and pencil. Quickly, Gwen went over to the girl.

"Nice drawing," Gwen said as the girl began to doodle.

"Thanks," said the girl with a sigh.

"What's your name?" asked Gwen.

← THE DOODLE THAT GWEN TRACED FROM THE BOOK

"Pam." She sighed again. "I love Lhasa apsos. My aunt has one, but my parents won't let me have a dog."

"Gee, Pam, that's too bad," said Gwen. "Is that why you cut their pictures out of library books?"

Pam turned green. She dropped her
pad and pencil and ran.

"Hey, come back," cried Gwen. She
ran after her.

"Jill! Jill!! I found her. HELP!"

Jill came running, dragging Fletcher behind her. They chased the girl all over the dog show, past the Irish setters, the Old English sheepdogs and Airedales.

They cornered her next to the fox terriers.

"You cut those pictures out of the library books," accused Gwen. "That's against the law."

"And a creepy, selfish thing to do," said Jill.

"I couldn't help myself," said Pam. "My parents got so sick of hearing me ask for a dog that they wouldn't even buy me a book with pictures of dogs. So I started going to the library. First, I was going to cut out just one little picture for my wall, then . . ."

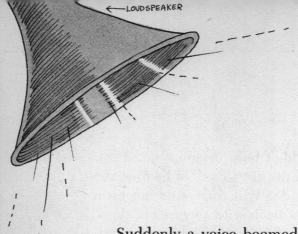

←LOUDSPEAKER

Suddenly a voice boomed out over the loudspeaker. "The basset hound competition will begin in two minutes in the main ring."

"Come on," yelled Jill, waking Fletcher up. They hurried to the main ring. They made Pam go with them.

CLOSE-UP
OF FLETCHER'S
UNUSUAL
MARKINGS
←

Fletcher did not win first prize. The judge said his stomach slumped too much. However, he won $25 for the most unusual markings.

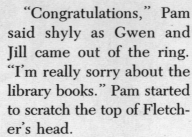

"Congratulations," Pam said shyly as Gwen and Jill came out of the ring. "I'm really sorry about the library books." Pam started to scratch the top of Fletcher's head.

"You really love dogs, don't you?" said Gwen.

"Fletcher's wonderful," said Pam. "I think basset hounds are almost as nice as Lhasa apsos."

Jill grinned.

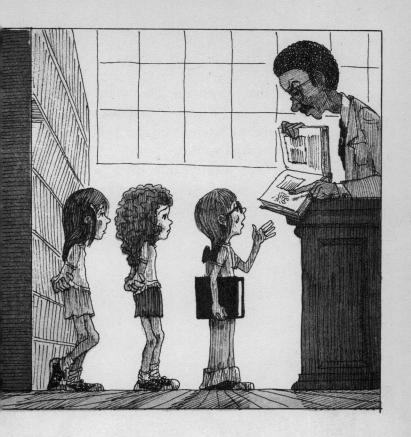

That afternoon, Gwen and Jill took Pam, the books, and Fletcher to the library. Mr. Hobart was very serious. He told Pam her parents would have to pay for the books. He made her promise she would never cut a picture out of a library book again. Then Mr. Hobart went outside to look at Fletcher's award-winning markings. He was very impressed.

Later that afternoon, Pam went with Gwen, Jill, and Fletcher to a pet store. They bought Fletcher a water bed with the $25 he had won.

"I bet he's wanted that since he was a puppy," said Gwen as Fletcher fell asleep, slowly bobbing up and down in his new bed.

PAM

JILL, FILLI
THE WAT
BED